W9-AMR-465

For Lucy and Ruben, with love
— D.H.

For Tim and Noah
— J.C.

Text copyright © 2001 by Diana Hendry
Illustrations copyright © 2001 by Jane Chapman
All rights reserved.

CIP Data is available.

Published in the United States 2002 by Dutton Children's Books,
a division of Penguin Putnam Books for Young Readers
345 Hudson Street, New York, NY 10014
www.penguinputnam.com

Originally published in Great Britain 2001 by Little Tiger Press,
an imprint of Magi Publications, London
Typography by Alan Carr · Printed in Italy
First American Edition · ISBN 0-525-46825-0
2 4 6 8 10 9 7 5 3 1

The Very BUSY Day

by **Diana Hendry** · illustrated by **Jane Chapman**

DUTTON CHILDREN'S BOOKS · NEW YORK

It was a sunny day, and Big Mouse had decided to work in the garden. Little Mouse had other plans.

SWISH!

Little Mouse sat on the swing, wearing his sun hat. "There's a lot of digging to do," said Big Mouse. "Come and help me, Little Mouse." "I'm too busy to help," said Little Mouse. "I'm dreaming up something." And he swung up and down, up and down.

"You could plant these seeds," Big Mouse offered. "If you cover them with soil, they'll grow into flowers."

SWISH!

"Umm," said Little Mouse. "I'm busy thinking about my dream." "Busy doing nothing," grumbled Big Mouse.

WHEEE!

Little Mouse flew off the swing and into the wheelbarrow. He lay and gazed at the sky.
 "I need that wheelbarrow for the weeds," said Big Mouse. "And look at the mess you've made."

Big Mouse tipped Little Mouse
out onto the grass. "Please,
Little Mouse, I need some help."
"I'm very busy," cried Little
Mouse, and he ran off
to pick some daisies.

Big Mouse picked up all the weeds. He mopped his brow and stretched his back.

"Phew, it's hot," he puffed. . . .

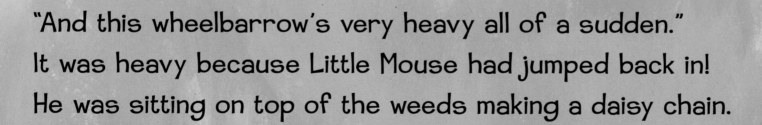

"And this wheelbarrow's very heavy all of a sudden."
It was heavy because Little Mouse had jumped back in!
He was sitting on top of the weeds making a daisy chain.

"I'm not pushing you *and* the weeds," said
Big Mouse indignantly. "Out you go! Come
and help me take the weeds to the dump."
    Little Mouse scrambled out of the
wheelbarrow, but he didn't help Big Mouse.

He picked lots and lots
of clover instead.

HUFF!

PUFF!

Big Mouse pushed the wheelbarrow to
the dump by himself, muttering angrily.

Then Big Mouse went to find his rake.
He couldn't see Little Mouse anywhere.
"Come on, Little Mouse," he called.
"There's a little rake here
for you, too."

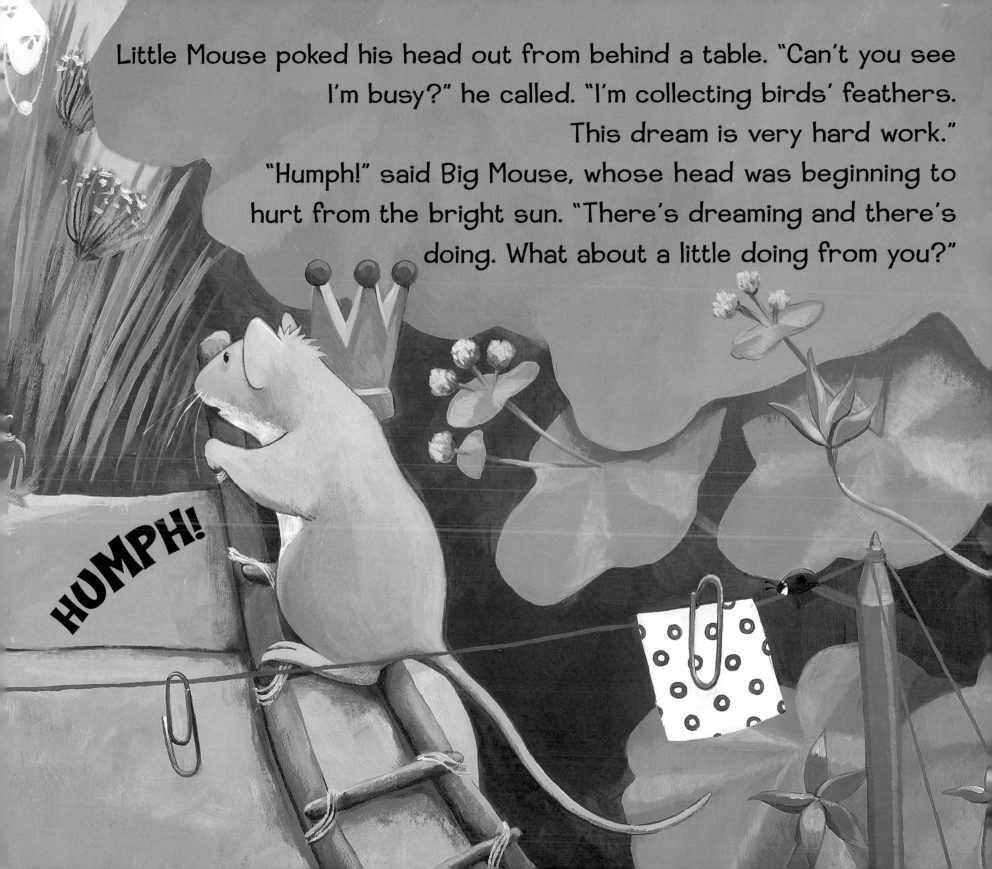

Little Mouse poked his head out from behind a table. "Can't you see I'm busy?" he called. "I'm collecting birds' feathers. This dream is very hard work."

"Humph!" said Big Mouse, whose head was beginning to hurt from the bright sun. "There's dreaming and there's doing. What about a little doing from you?"

HUMPH!

Little Mouse had found three
snowy white feathers.
He laid them carefully
on the doorstep.

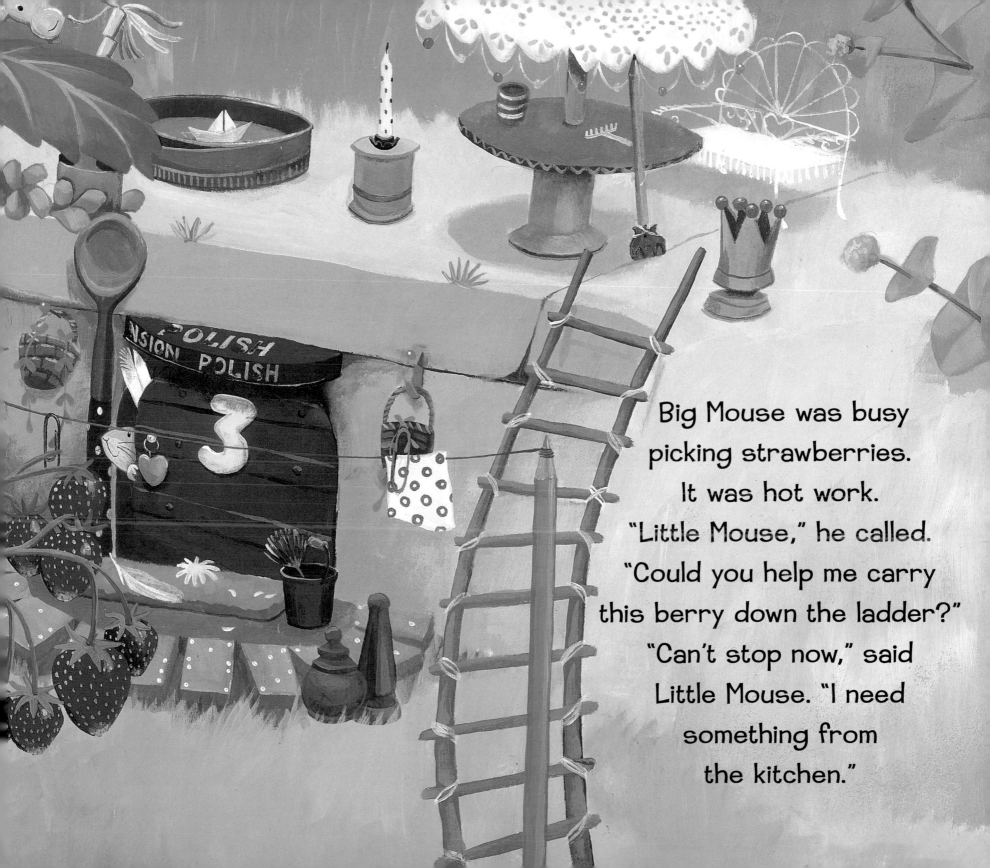

Big Mouse was busy
picking strawberries.
It was hot work.
"Little Mouse," he called.
"Could you help me carry
this berry down the ladder?"
"Can't stop now," said
Little Mouse. "I need
something from
the kitchen."

Now Big Mouse's head
really hurt, and with each
throb of pain, he felt more
annoyed at Little Mouse.
"What is he doing now?"
he grumbled.

Little Mouse rushed out into the yard. "Big Mouse, Big Mouse," he called. "Look what I've made for you."

"It's your very own
sun hat! To wear to our picnic."
"Oh," said Big Mouse, surprised and
still grumpy. But he put it on his head.
It did keep the sun out of his eyes.
"Did you say *picnic*?" he asked.

"Well," said Little Mouse, "we've both been working very hard. I thought we should take a break and eat the strawberries we picked." Big Mouse sighed. But he couldn't help admiring his new hat. It was special—too special to wear just for gardening. . . .

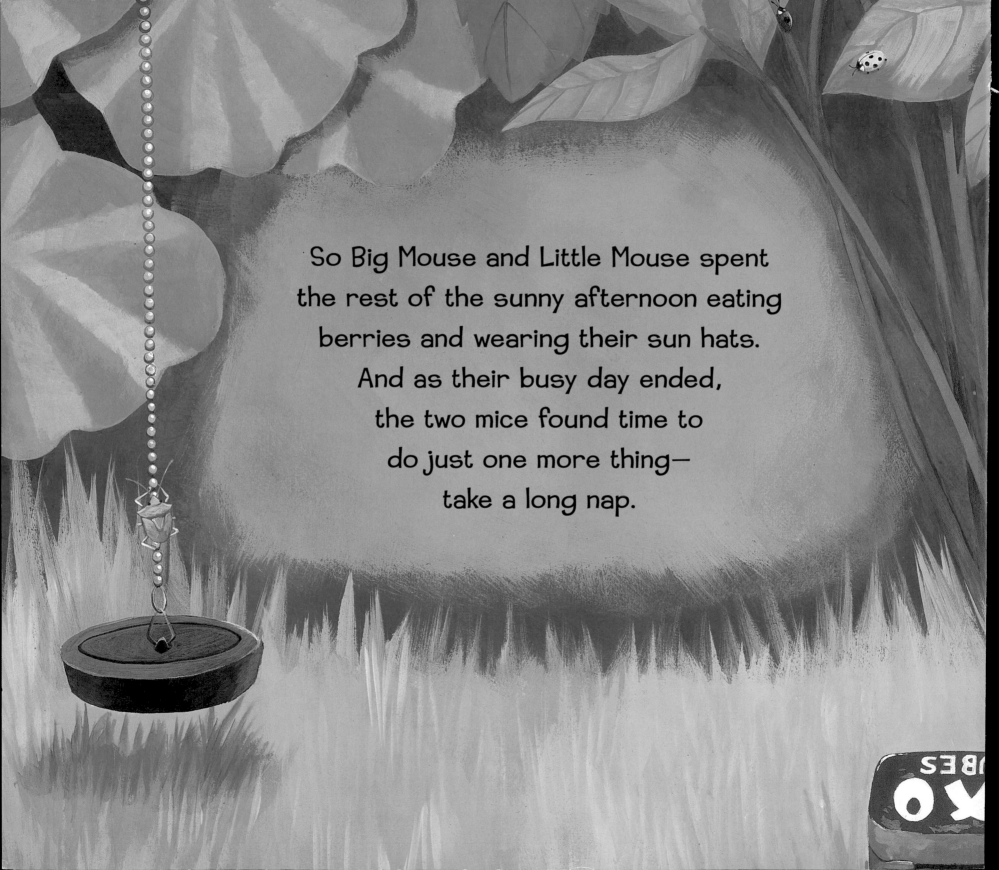

So Big Mouse and Little Mouse spent
the rest of the sunny afternoon eating
berries and wearing their sun hats.
And as their busy day ended,
the two mice found time to
do just one more thing—
take a long nap.